Expl... Friends or Foes?

by Mrs. Clausen-Grace's class
with Tony Stead

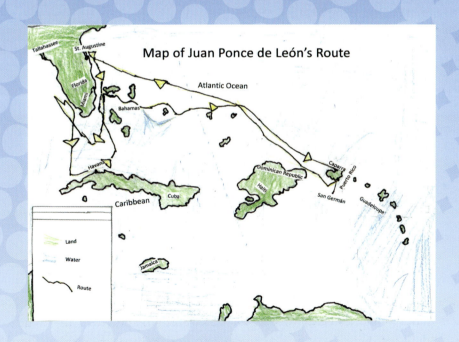

Map of Juan Ponce de León's Route

Tallahassee
St. Augustine
Florida
Miami
Bahamas
Atlantic Ocean
Havana
Caribbean
Cuba
Dominican Republic
Haiti
San Germán
Caparra
Puerto Rico
Guadeloupe
Jamaica

Land
Water
Route

capstone
classroom

Introduction

by Michael and Ande

There are many different theories about explorers being friends or foes. No one knows the real answer, but this fifth grade class has been researching it for months.

We have read books and watched videos about explorers. We even went to St. Augustine to study the Spanish explorers. We also got a tour of the Castillo de San Marcos, a Spanish fort.

In this book, there are two sections. In the first section, there are seven persuasive essays about the explorers being friends. In the second section, there are seven persuasive essays about the explorers being foes. When you are done reading, you can decide what you think about the explorers being friends or foes.

Explorers as Friends

by Ty

I think that European explorers played a vital part in creating our nation. I will cover two main points that prove this statement true. The first is that Álvar Núñez Cabeza de Vaca was helped by American Indians. The second is that the Timucua tribe and the Spanish lived peacefully together.

In *Spanish Explorers: Researching American History,* author Pat Perrin claims that when European explorer Cabeza de Vaca landed in Galveston, Texas, he and his crew were fortunate to know a friendly American Indian tribe nearby. After the Indians fed the explorer and his men, they tried to put Cabeza de Vaca's ship back in the water, but it capsized, killing some of the crew. Miraculously, this did not start a war. Instead, the American Indians helped the Europeans get ready for the upcoming winter.

Jim Gallagher explains in his book *Hernando de Soto and the Exploration of Florida,* that the Spanish and the Timucua tribe lived peacefully together. This is because

Hernando de Soto gave gifts to the Timucuan king when he found the Spaniard Juan Ortiz living with the Timucua. The king could have executed Ortiz, but instead he took him in.

American Indians helped Cabeza de Vaca and Hernando de Soto. All in all, this proves that American Indians thought of the explorers as friends.

Explorers as Friends

by Kevin

Bent on killing and destruction—that's what some people think about the European explorers. But I believe European explorers were a positive force that helped start the founding of our nation.

According to the film *Explorers of the World: French Explorers,* the French were friends with the Indians so the French could have allies in the New World. The Spanish gave gifts to Indians. People think that the English mingled with the Croatian tribe when times got rough for the Roanoke colony. This is one reason I think the European explorers were friends to the American Indians.

The Europeans colonized the land they owned. Spain laid claim to Mexico and Florida. England owned the eastern coast, and France quickly colonized the core of the Americas. They then set up settlements so they could start searching for gold, silver, rubies, and emeralds. The English got a late start, but were successful in the New World. In the film *Explorers of the World: English Explorers,* the colony of Jamestown was started by English explorer Sir Walter Raleigh.

Lastly, the Europeans found ways to trade with the American Indians. More specifically, the explorers had discovered the St. Johns River with the Huron and Algonquian Indians. These two tribes were intent on trading with the explorers. This opened up another river that led to trading with the American Indians and helped the explorers get fresh provisions during winter, which helped the colonies thrive. This is the third and final reason I think the explorers were helpful to the Indians.

All in all, the explorers were helpful. Through their colonization and trading, America thrived. Consequently, the explorers were a positive force at the start of our beloved nation.

Sir Walter Raleigh's journeys sparked the settlement of Jamestown.

Explorers as Friends

by Ryan

Imagine receiving gifts from people you hardly know! Explorers helped to form our nation. They were also friendly and peaceful to the American Indians. Let's go to the New World and see acts of kindness along the way.

Look to the south. That's Pedro Menéndez de Avilés searching for his son Juan Menéndez de Avilés who got stuck in a storm. According to one source, Pedro Menéndez de Avilés searched up and down the Florida coastline. The search was unsuccessful, but he made peace with the tribes he met while looking for his son.

Despite killing the Indians, Hernando de Soto also tried to make peace. Although some say explorers killed Indians, the Indians actually tried to kill off explorers so they could have their land back. According to Jim Gallagher's book *Hernando de Soto and the Exploration of Florida,* de Soto also gave native chiefs gifts.

Tamara Green explains in her book *Juan Ponce de León,* that Spanish lawmakers thought the American Indians were like kids and gave explorers the right to enslave them, but the lawmakers also told explorers to treat Indians kindly. The French explorers befriended the tribes so they could have allies in the New World. The enslaved Indians tried to kill or attack explorers. Making peace was important for explorers who traded and needed corn.

Explorers were a positive force to the forming of our nation. The peacefulness helped explorers thrive in the New World. These are some of the reasons why explorers were friends to the American Indians.

Explorers as Friends

by Kayla

Would you like to live without a way to communicate over long distances or tell time? I didn't think so. The European explorers helped the American Indians by offering them a new way to live. Europeans brought useful tools and made peace with the Indians. They also built settlements and traded their tools with the Indians. I am very thankful that the explorers came to our world.

The Indians and the European explorers got along so well that they became trading partners. The Indian chief is trading crops for beads and copper.

When Christopher Columbus found new land, he already had sailors, soldiers, and skilled workmen waiting to get off his ship and build colonies and settlements. According to the film *Explorers of the World: French Explorers,* the settlements helped because the explorers and the American Indians became trading partners. Since the American Indians lived nearby, it gave them a chance to observe and learn from the explorers.

The explorers also brought many inventions with them, including the printing press, the water clock, and gunpowder. According to Donna Trembinski in her book *Famous People of the Middle Ages,* these inventions changed Indians' lives. The printing press helped get messages out quickly. The water clock could be used to find out where the sun, moon, and stars were. Although the explorers used gunpowder for war, it was also used for fun things like fireworks. All in all, the explorers brought many useful tools and inventions to the Indians.

Now you can see why the explorers were friends to the American Indians. They built colonies and settlements and brought many inventions to the New World. The American Indians' lives changed because of the explorers' helping hands.

Explorers as Friends

by Oliver

If explorers didn't explore the New World, they wouldn't have found where we now live. Here are some other reasons why I think explorers were friends.

The explorers wrote about their journeys. Joan Holub states in her book *Who Was Marco Polo?* that Marco Polo wrote books about his journeys. In these books, Polo would include maps and share the routes to different locations.

To add to that, the book *Famous People of the Middle Ages* by Donna Trembinski explains that explorers would bring inventions with them, like the printing press. During the explorers' time, using a printing press meant not having to write everything by hand. Trembinski goes on to say that explorers brought weapons that helped the American Indians.

I think Europeans were helpful when they made new colonies because this gave them more space. Otherwise, Europe would have had too many people and would have become overpopulated. Colonies were also helpful because if families were attacked, they could get a boat and food and go to another colony for safety.

Last of all, if other countries ran out of materials, people could go to America to get more. For example, when Europe was out of gold, Europeans went to America and got more.

Many people say that explorers were insane and terrorized villages. But if they didn't exist, we would live somewhere far away from where we live now because they would not have explored this land.

Explorers as Friends

by Ethan

People have different opinions about whether explorers were bad or good. I think explorers were good because they helped form our nation. They were helpful for several reasons.

Columbus wanted to go west to India, but the islands near Central America blocked his way. Columbus thought he was in India, so he told the king he found the west passage to India. In our textbook, the authors claim that when Columbus returned to Spain, he told other explorers about this new land, and they traveled there too.

In order to live in the New World, be safe, and trade, European explorers had to make new colonies. As stated in the book *René-Robert Cavelier, Sieur de La Salle* by Jim Hargrove, the explorers traded beads for fur with the American Indians. The Indians traded bread, yams, corn, fish, gold trinkets, and cotton hammocks for red caps, brass belts, and glass beads. Explorers traded many things as a way to make friends with the American Indians and stay safe while building colonies.

Explorers were good for our nation. They built new colonies, which led to trading and the creation of America.

Explorers as Friends

by Anthony

I believe that the explorers were helpful in forming our country and will explain three reasons why in detail.

The state that you are living in may be one of the first colonies of America. The explorers established these first colonies. The English established New York and North Carolina as colonies. According to Trish Kline in her book *Ponce de León,* Ponce de León established Florida as a colony.

The explorers also became friends with the American Indians. For example, Hernando de Soto became friends with the Timucua tribe, Columbus traded with the Taíno tribe, and Giovanni da Verrazzano became trading allies with American Indians.

The explorers did kind things for the Indians. In Tamara Green's book *Juan Ponce de León,* she explains that Ponce de León protected the Taíno tribe from their enemies, the Caribs. And Hernando de Soto gave gifts to the Timucuan leader. In the film *Explorers of the World: French Explorers,* we learn that Giovanni da Verrazzano took an Indian chief's sons on his boat to show them France.

Imagine that you are an explorer sailing in a boat and hoping you will find gold. But you don't find any gold. Instead you establish the first colonies of the New World. You become friends with the American Indians and help them in many ways. These are the reasons why I think the explorers were friends not foes.

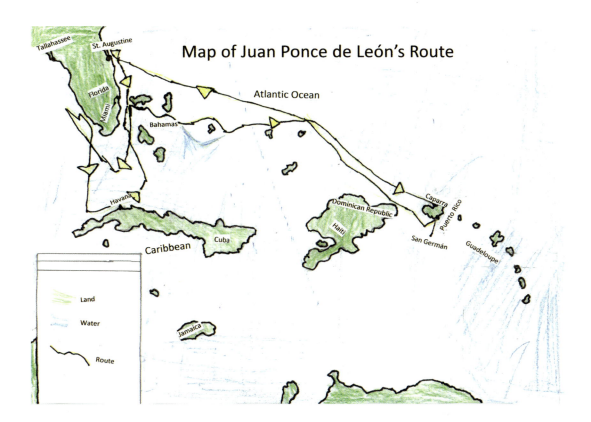

Map of Juan Ponce de León's Route

Explorers as Foes

by Rei and Hannah

European explorers were antagonists to the American Indians and spread unknown or incurable diseases. They also cost many Indians their lives in deadly, bloody wars. These are a couple of reasons why we think European explorers were a disgrace to our country.

To begin with, European explorers were enemies to the American Indians. As noted in *Explorers* by Dennis Fradin, Spaniard Francisco Pizarro killed thousands of Inca Indians and destroyed their culture. Many explorers held American Indians captive and used them for hard labor. Killing American Indians and destroying their culture are just two ways that the European explorers were unkind to the tribes that lived in the New World.

Another reason is that the explorers started deadly wars that caused many people to lose their lives. Hernán Cortés stormed the Tabascan territory, taking the lives of thousands of Tabascans. After slaughtering them, he also ordered the only barely living Tabascans to bring him all of the town's valuables, describes Jeff Donaldson-Forbes in his book *Hernán Cortés*. Also, the European explorers burned and robbed the houses and took all the crops, causing the American Indians to die from hunger. The explorers were greedy and were bent on getting everything they wanted.

European explorers also brought diseases like measles, scurvy, and smallpox to the New World. The illnesses passed from person to person and wiped out entire tribes. According to our textbook, these diseases diminished many tribes. It was the Indians' worst fear and biggest danger. If the Europeans had not come to the New World, the American Indians would not have had to suffer those sicknesses.

Imagine watching a loved one die from war or disease. This is what the Indians had to deal with when the European explorers invaded their territory. Even though the explorers built colonies and started trade, they were ruthless and caused much harm and pain to the Indians.

Explorers as Foes

by Savannah and Jailyn

Imagine your whole town being destroyed and the people being sold. That's what happened to the American Indians when the Europeans came to their land. The explorers were merciless foes to the Indians. The explorers killed, were cruel to, and forced the Indians into slavery.

The explorers were so cruel to the American Indians that they took away their freedom and their families. For example, Jacques Cartier, the French explorer, captured two teen Indians along with their tribe chief, as recounted in the film *Explorers of the World: French Explorers*. Many European colonists forced American Indians to work on farms. The colonists liked to use strong, fast teenagers.

While it may be true that some explorers were trying to be friends with the American Indians, most explorers were destructive to Indian lands. In Betsy and Giulio Maestro's book *Exploration and Conquest,* we learn that Hernando de Soto and his men set fire to entire villages and took all the Indians' food. They also murdered thousands of Indians. The ones left alive were enslaved by the Europeans. In addition, Juan Ponce de León started a war against the Carib tribe, as detailed in Deborah Crisfield's book *The Travels of Juan Ponce de León.* Furthermore, when Columbus came to the New World, he and his men felt like they could do whatever they wanted. They took the American Indians' land, their things, and even worse, their lives. As you can see, the European explorers were foes.

statue of a Carib Indian

Explorers as Foes

by Skyler

Have you ever experienced being someone's enemy? I know that the American Indians experienced this. There are a lot of reasons why the explorers were foes to the Indians.

Explorers used the native Floridians as slaves. The American Indians were forced to carry the soldiers' equipment. Taíno Indians were sold as slaves or killed after Christopher Columbus transported them to Spain.

European explorers and native Floridians warred. The Indians fought the explorers because they were on Indian land and invading Indian property. Juan Ponce de León won a war against the Carib tribe. The Calusas attacked Ponce de León and his men, shooting de León in the leg with a poisonous arrow, which killed him. The Calusas killed him because they were tired of the Europeans living on their land. This fight turned into war, according to Dan Harmon in his book *Juan Ponce de León and the Search for the Fountain of Youth*.

The European explorers invaded Indian land. The explorers were cruel to the native Floridians by using them as slaves, and the explorers started wars with the Indians. Now you know why explorers were foes.

The map on the bottom left shows Ponce de León's path and where he was killed. The picture above shows de León being shot by a Calusa arrow.

Explorers as Foes

by Caleb and Yanik

Murderous. Bloodthirsty. Destructive. These names all apply to the European explorers. European explorers killed American Indians like one ant colony fights another ant colony. European explorers were murderous enemies to the American Indians and our nation.

Hernando de Soto, like many other explorers, was murderous. In John W. Kincheloe's article "Earliest American Explorers: Adventure and Survival," he states that one of the reasons so many American Indians died is because the explorers brought diseases to America that the American Indians could not cure. The explorers also slaughtered the Indians. For example, thousands of Indians died in a war with Juan Ponce de León.

When the European explorers "found" America, they made the American Indians slaves. The Indians were forced to build houses for the explorers. Also, Hernando de Soto captured Indian prisoners after a battle in Peru.

Francisco Vázquez de Coronado led an expedition to steal gold from the seven cities of gold. Pánfilo de Narváez captured an Indian chief, and Hernando de Soto captured a Timucuan chief to steal his gold.

As you can see, the European explorers were bloodthirsty people intent on killing the American Indians. Explorers were wicked because they killed Indians, established slavery in America, and stole from people.

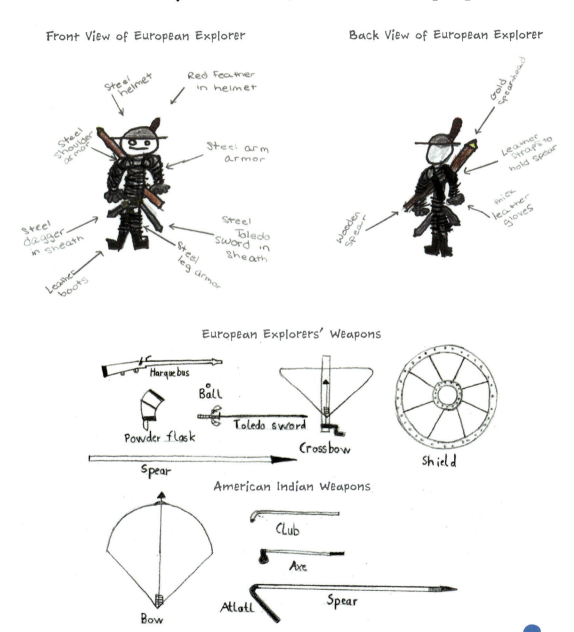

Front View of European Explorer

Steel helmet
Red Feather in helmet
Steel shoulder armor
Steel arm armor
Steel dagger in sheath
Steel Toledo sword in sheath
Leather boots
Steel leg armor

Back View of European Explorer

Gold spearhead
Leather straps to hold spear
thick leather gloves
Wooden spear

European Explorers' Weapons

Harquebus
Ball
Powder flask
Toledo sword
Crossbow
Spear
Shield

American Indian Weapons

Club
Axe
Bow
Atlatl
Spear

Explorers as Foes

by Anistonk

Imagine walking back home to your village and it's up in flames. Everything is gone, and all your friends and family are dead. This is an example of what European explorers did to the American Indians. The explorers killed, stole from, and enslaved them. For these reasons, it's obvious the explorers were foes of the American Indians.

Hernando de Soto brought pain and misery to tribes he met by raiding them, as reported by Betsy and Giulio Maestro in the book *Exploration and Conquest.* Explorers would steal food from the villages. They would also steal the Indians and turn them into slaves. Before they left, the explorers would burn the village.

In *Spanish Explorers: Researching American History,* author Pat Perrin claims that American Indians would kill European explorers for fun. The explorers were so mean to the Indians, that the Indians started killing the explorers. By capturing and terrorizing Indians, the explorers brought the killings on themselves. I personally think the American Indians killed explorers for revenge.

Although European explorers helped with making the United States, they killed innocent American Indians. Explorers didn't just kill Indians, they enslaved them too. Explorers captured Indians and then traded them for food. Our textbook asserts that Spanish soldiers threatened Indians to make them carry heavy bags and equipment.

As you can see, European explorers were enemies of the American Indians. How dare the explorers kill, steal, and enslave them? The explorers were brutal killers.

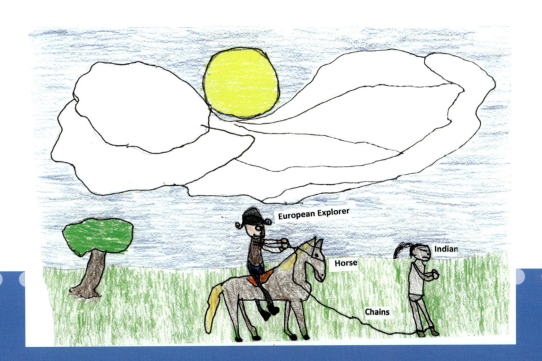

Explorers as Foes

by Aidan and Grant

Imagine you came back to your village and it was raided, burned, and destroyed. We believe the explorers were terrorists who attacked and destroyed American Indian tribes and families. They killed, robbed, and caused many tribes to become extinct. The explorers were destructive, murderous people. We can name many reasons why the explorers were foes.

One reason is that they caused death and destruction. They stole things from villages, such as weapons and food, states Peggy Pancella in her book *Hernando de Soto*. Hernando de Soto and Pánfilo de Narváez enslaved Indians. The explorers warred with Indians, killing many per battle.

Another reason explorers were foes is because they brought diseases such as smallpox and measles that spread quickly, according to Elizabeth Weiss Vollstadt in her book *Florida*.

The last reason we believe the explorers were foes is because they robbed the American Indians and made them slaves. In the book *De Soto,* Ann Heinrichs says that the Cofitachequi chief gave de Soto plenty of gifts. Since the tribe had nothing de Soto wanted, he took the chief prisoner. He did this so the tribe would give him food.

In conclusion, these greedy killers were mean to the American Indians: killing, kidnapping, burning villages, and causing many tribes to become extinct. The explorers got rid of the Indians' lifestyles and traditions too. As we said in the beginning, the explorers were terrorists.

Explorers as Foes

by Ashlynn

What if you came home and found out that your family had been captured? That's what happened when European explorers came to North America. European explorers were invaders to the American Indians.

Indian land and crops were shared throughout most of the tribes in North America. American Indians only used what they needed, but when European explorers came, they stole food when they were hungry and took land for houses. Indian land was especially loved for its fresh and moist soil; long, fish-filled streams; plenty of large killable animals (such as deer); and tall, sky-reaching trees to make houses and fires. The European explorers even burned trees down to make room for large houses.

Explorers killed American Indians with their rifles and harsh diseases. Most Indians in Florida died because of illnesses such as smallpox and measles. These diseases were unknown to the American Indians before Spanish explorers came to Florida. These diseases were untreatable because Indians didn't know what they were.

Some explorers, such as the Spanish, wanted slaves to do their work. Pánfilo de Narváez took Chief Utica hostage after Narváez found gold in Chief Utica's territory. Narváez chopped Chief Utica's nose clean off, reports Pat Perrin in the book *Spanish Explorers: Researching American History*. Some slaves had to clean up the stables, and others had to build houses for the European explorers.

As you can plainly see, European explorers were invaders to American Indians and North America. They took Indian land and crops, killed off tribes, and made some Indians into slaves. If you were alive during this time, how would you feel if you were an American Indian?

When Columbus and his men found the New World, the men rejoiced. Columbus thought that the land he found was India so he called the men there Indians.

Conclusion

by Emily and Sarah

You have read essays about explorers being friends or foes. Oliver thinks explorers were friends because they invented helpful and useful tools such as the printing press. But Grant and Aidan believe explorers were foes because they caused death and destruction.

Now it's your turn to decide whether or not explorers were friends or foes. Do you agree with Hannah and Rei, who said the explorers were foes because they started wars? Or do you agree with Kevin who said that the explorers were friends because they colonized America? Do you think explorers were helpful or were they murderers? What makes you believe your statement?

American Indians drumming at a powwow